At the check-in counter, the agent stamped Mickey's ticket and then Minnie's.

Goofy looked and looked for his, and finally found it stuck between two ham sandwiches he had packed for a snack.

The ticket agent stamped the ticket. "Now, don't lose this," she warned Goofy.

Goofy thought hard. "I know!" he exclaimed. "I'll put it inside my pilot's hat. That's really safe."

He tucked the ticket snugly inside the hat.

Just then, as a group of pilots hurried into the airline terminal,
a stiff breeze blew Goofy's hat right off his head—*whoosh!*
"Stop that hat!" Goofy yelled, racing after it.

As Goofy chased his runaway hat, he bumped into the pilots, knocking their hats and flight bags in every direction.

"Gawrsh! I'm sorry!" Goofy apologized as he helped everyone pick up their belongings.

The pilots smiled, placed their hats back on their heads, and hurried off to their planes.

Goofy picked up the last hat and looked inside. "Oh, no!" he cried. "One of those pilots took my hat by mistake! And my ticket's in it!"

"Don't worry, Goofy," said Mickey. "We'll help you find the pilot who has your hat."

Mickey knocked on the door of the air traffic control tower. Inside, people with radios were telling the pilots when to take off and land their planes.

"Could you please use your radios to ask the pilots if one of them has Goofy's hat and ticket?" Mickey asked.

Minnie put her bags through the X-ray machine and hurried down
a long hall to the boarding area. She saw hundreds of people getting
on and off planes, but she didn't see a single pilot anywhere.

Meanwhile, Goofy spotted a pilot walking toward the baggage claim area. Goofy ran after the pilot, but he tripped and fell—*klunk*—onto a baggage conveyor loaded with suitcases.

Around and around Goofy whirled until his head was spinning!

BAGGAGE CLAIM

Goofy staggered off the conveyor and stumbled through a door
that led to the edge of the airfield. A plane was taxiing past slowly.

Through the cockpit window, Goofy saw a pilot
wearing a hat that looked like his.

"Stop! Stop!" Goofy shouted, waving his arms.

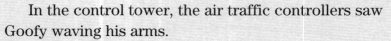

In the control tower, the air traffic controllers saw Goofy waving his arms.

"Goofy is signaling us to stop that plane," one of the controllers said.

She radioed the pilot who was flying the plane.
Quickly, the startled pilot stepped on the brakes.

Then Goofy saw another plane going by, and another, and another. All the pilots were wearing hats like his!

"Stop! Stop!" Goofy shouted, waving his arms again.

The traffic controllers radioed all the pilots to stop their planes. Soon Goofy had brought the whole airport to a standstill.

Suddenly one of the pilots began waving at Goofy.

"I heard the control tower's announcement," the pilot shouted. "I've got your hat! Come and get it!"

Goofy ran up to the door of the plane, and the pilot handed him his hat. Luckily, the ticket was still tucked safely inside!

Finally, it was time for Mickey, Minnie, and Goofy to board their plane. The flight attendant tore off part of Goofy's ticket and handed the rest back to him.

"That's your return ticket," Mickey explained to Goofy as they sat down and buckled their seat belts. "If you lose it, you won't be able to fly home."

"Don't worry," Goofy said. "This time I'm putting it in a really safe place—my shoe!"

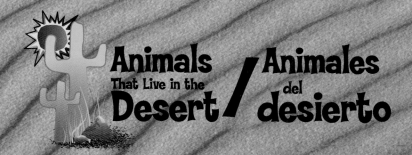

Rattlesnakes/
Serpientes de cascabel

JoAnn Early Macken

Reading consultant/Consultora de lectura:
Susan Nations, M. Ed., author, literacy coach,
consultant/autora, tutora de alfabetización, consultora

WR WEEKLY READER
EARLY LEARNING LIBRARY

Please visit our web site at: www.earlyliteracy.cc
For a free color catalog describing Weekly Reader® Early Learning Library's list
of high-quality books, call 1-877-445-5824 (USA) or 1-800-387-3178 (Canada).
Weekly Reader® Early Learning Library's fax: (414) 336-0164.

Library of Congress Cataloging-in-Publication Data available upon request from publisher.
Fax (414) 336-0157 for the attention of the Publishing Records Department.

ISBN 0-8368-4843-8 (lib. bdg.)
ISBN 0-8368-4850-0 (softcover)

This edition first published in 2006 by
Weekly Reader® Early Learning Library
A Member of the WRC Media Family of Companies
330 West Olive Street, Suite 100
Milwaukee, WI 53212 USA

Art direction: Tammy West
Cover design and page layout: Kami Koenig
Picture research: Diane Laska-Swanke
Translators: Tatiana Acosta and Guillermo Gutiérrez

Picture credits: Cover, p. 11 © Joe McDonald/Visuals Unlimited; p. 5 © Richard Day/
Daybreak Imagery; p. 7 © Gerold and Cynthia Merker/Visuals Unlimited; pp. 9, 17,
21 © John Cancalosi/naturepl.com; p. 13 © Dr. Nathan Cohen/Visuals Unlimited;
p. 15 © David Welling/naturepl.com; p. 19 © Jeff Foott/naturepl.com

Printed in the United States of America

1 2 3 4 5 6 7 8 9 09 08 07 06 05

Note to Educators and Parents

Reading is such an exciting adventure for young children! They are beginning to integrate their oral language skills with written language. To encourage children along the path to early literacy, books must be colorful, engaging, and interesting; they should invite the young reader to explore both the print and the pictures.

Animals That Live in the Desert is a new series designed to help children read about creatures that make their homes in dry places. Each book explains where a different desert animal lives, what it eats, and how it adapts to its arid environment.

Each book is specially designed to support the young reader in the reading process. The familiar topics are appealing to young children and invite them to read — and reread — again and again. The full-color photographs and enhanced text further support the student during the reading process.

In addition to serving as wonderful picture books in schools, libraries, homes, and other places where children learn to love reading, these books are specifically intended to be read within an instructional guided reading group. This small group setting allows beginning readers to work with a fluent adult model as they make meaning from the text. After children develop fluency with the text and content, the book can be read independently. Children and adults alike will find these books supportive, engaging, and fun!

— Susan Nations, M.Ed., author, literacy coach,
and consultant in literacy development

Nota para los maestros y los padres

¡Leer es una aventura tan emocionante para los niños pequeños! A esta edad están comenzando a integrar su manejo del lenguaje oral con el lenguaje escrito. Para animar a los niños en el camino de la lectura incipiente, los libros deben ser coloridos, estimulantes e interesantes; deben invitar a los jóvenes lectores a explorar la letra impresa y las ilustraciones.

Animales del desierto es una nueva colección diseñada para que los niños lean textos sobre animales que viven en lugares muy secos. Cada libro explica dónde vive un animal del desierto, qué come y cómo se adapta a su árido medio ambiente.

Cada libro está especialmente diseñado para ayudar a los jóvenes lectores en el proceso de lectura. Los temas familiares llaman la atención de los niños y los invitan a leer —y releer— una y otra vez. Las fotografías a todo color y el tamaño de la letra ayudan aún más al estudiante en el proceso de lectura.

Además de servir como maravillosos libros ilustrados en escuelas, bibliotecas, hogares y otros lugares donde los niños aprenden a amar la lectura, estos libros han sido especialmente concebidos para ser leídos en un grupo de lectura guiada. Este contexto permite que los lectores incipientes trabajen con un adulto que domina la lectura mientras van determinando el significado del texto. Una vez que los niños dominan el texto y el contenido, el libro puede ser leído de manera independiente. ¡Estos libros les resultarán útiles, estimulantes y divertidos a niños y a adultos por igual!

— Susan Nations, M.Ed., autora/tutora de alfabetización/
consultora de desarrollo de la lectura

Rattlesnakes are known as **rattlers**. They are named for the sound they make. The sound is a warning. If you hear it, watch out!

- - - - - - - - - - - - - - -

A las serpientes de cascabel se las conoce como **cascabeles**. Se las llama así por el sonido que hacen. El sonido es una advertencia. Si lo escuchas, ¡ten cuidado!

4

A snake's rattle is made of hard, dry scales. The snake shakes its tail, and the scales buzz. The snake is about to bite!

El cascabel de esta serpiente está formado por escamas duras y secas. La serpiente mueve la cola y las escamas suenan. ¡La serpiente está a punto de morder!

rattle/
cascabel

7

Many rattlers are black, brown, and yellow. These colors make them hard to see. They are the colors of the desert.

- - - - - - - - - - - - -

Muchas cascabeles son negras, color café y amarillas. Esos colores hacen que sea difícil verlas. Esos son los colores del desierto.

Rattlesnakes are pit vipers. A **viper** is a snake with long **fangs**, or teeth. **Venom**, or poison, flows through the fangs when the snake bites.

- - - - - - - - - - - - - - - -

Las cascabeles son víboras de fosa. Una **víbora** es una serpiente que tiene unos **colmillos**, o dientes, largos. Cuando la serpiente muerde, una ponzoña o **veneno** le sale por los colmillos.

fangs/
colmillos

11

Rattlers have **pits**, or holes, on their faces. They can sense heat. This sense helps rattlers find food.

Las serpientes de cascabel tienen unas **fosas**, o agujeros, en la cara. Con éstas, las cascabeles sienten el calor. Este sentido las ayuda a conseguir comida.

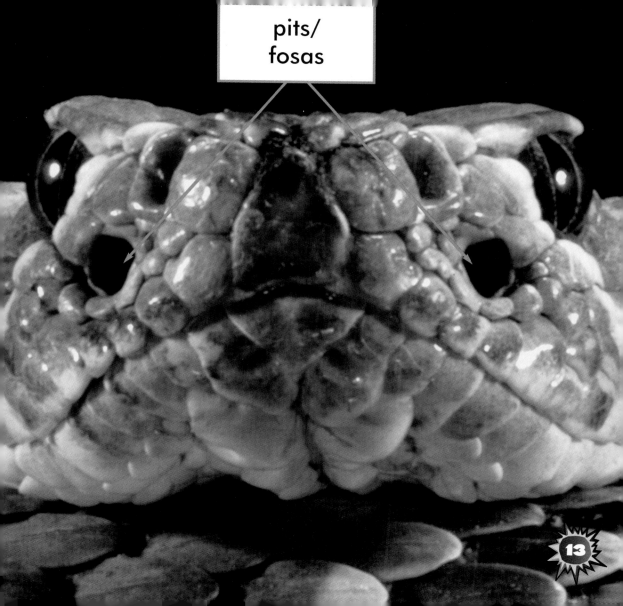

pits/
fosas

13

Rattlesnakes eat mice and rabbits. They eat birds and lizards. All snakes can open their mouths wide to eat.

- - - - - - - - - - - - -

Las cascabeles comen ratones y conejos. También comen pájaros y lagartos. Todas las serpientes pueden abrir mucho la boca cuando van a comer.

14

Baby rattlers are left on their own. They must find their own food. They must watch out! Birds and animals hunt for them!

‐ ‐ ‐ ‐ ‐ ‐ ‐ ‐ ‐ ‐ ‐ ‐ ‐

Las crías de cascabel crecen por su cuenta. Tienen que buscar su comida. ¡Y deben tener mucho cuidado! ¡Los pájaros y otros animales las buscan para comérselas!

Some snakes stay under the sand all day. They come out at night to hunt. Some snakes move sideways across the desert. They leave their tracks in the sand.

Algunas serpientes pasan todo el día bajo la arena. Por la noche, salen a cazar. Algunas serpientes se mueven lateralmente por el desierto. Dejan sus rastros en la arena.

tracks/
rastros

19

Some rattlers live where winters are cold. They may **hibernate**, or sleep through the winter. They come out in spring to eat.

- - - - - - - - - - - - - -

Algunas cascabeles viven en lugares con inviernos muy fríos. Pueden entonces **hibernar**, o dormir, durante el invierno. En la primavera, vuelven a salir para comer.

21

GLOSSARY

desert — a very dry area

fangs — long, hollow teeth

scales — thin, flat plates that cover the bodies of snakes, fish, and other animals

sideways — from one side to the other

warning — something that tells of danger

GLOSARIO

advertencia — algo que avisa de un peligro

colmillos — dientes largos y huecos

desierto — un área muy seca

escamas — placas delgadas y planas que cubren el cuerpo de las serpientes, los peces y otros animales

lateralmente — de lado

FOR MORE INFORMATION/ MÁS INFORMACIÓN

BOOKS IN ENGLISH

All About Rattlesnakes. All About (series). Jim Arnosky (Scholastic)

Rattlesnakes. Desert Animals (series). Emily Rose Townsend (Pebble Books)

LIBROS EN ESPAÑOL

La vida secreta de las serpientes. Lynn M. Stone (Rourke Publishing)

Snakes/Las serpientes. Animals I See at the Zoo/ Animales que veo en el zoológico (series). JoAnn Early Macken (Weekly Reader Early Learning Library)

INDEX

ÍNDICE

ABOUT THE AUTHOR

JoAnn Early Macken is the author of two rhyming picture books, *Sing-Along Song* and *Cats on Judy*, and many other nonfiction books for beginning readers. Her poems have appeared in several children's magazines. A graduate of the M.F.A. in Writing for Children and Young Adults program at Vermont College, she lives in Wisconsin with her husband and their two sons. Visit her Web site at www.joannmacken.com.

INFORMACIÓN SOBRE LA AUTORA

JoAnn Early Macken ha escrito dos libros de rimas con ilustraciones, *Sing-Along Song y Cats on Judy*, y muchos otros libros de no ficción para lectores incipientes. Sus poemas han sido publicados en varias revistas infantiles. JoAnn se graduó en el programa M.F.A. de Escritura para Niños y Jóvenes de Vermont College. Vive en Wisconsin con su esposo y sus dos hijos. Puedes visitar su página web: www.joannmacken.com